Mrs. Paddington
and the
Silver Mousetraps

A hair-raising history of women's hairstyles
in 18th-century London

Written by Gail Skroback Hennessey   Illustrated by Steve Cox

RED
CHAIR
•PRESS•

Mrs. MURIEL PADDINGTON sat in a high-backed chair staring at her reflection in the large, gold-leafed mirror in front of her. "I really need to get my thoughts together on how to wear my hair for this Saturday's Moonlight Ball."

Mrs. Paddington's hairdresser, Mrs. Blinkhorn, stood behind her, fussing with different suggestions. "Why not a solar system in your hair?" asked Mrs. Blinkhorn.

Mrs. Paddington frowned, "No, I have already done a solar system for Priscilla Abernathy's Spring Ball."

Mrs. Blinkhorn placed her hands into the air. "I've got it. Let's try a bird cage in your hair!"

"I would NEVER and I mean *never* do a bird cage in my hair again," began Mrs. Paddington. "Don't you remember when you placed a birdcage in my hairdo for the Summer Solstice Ball? The canary squawked and squawked and I couldn't sleep for days. And, when I fed the bird, it dropped the hulls from the sunflower seeds onto my face. One actually landed on my eyelash and scratched my eye."

"To make matters even worse, one of the hulls dropped beneath my nose. When I took a breath, the hull went up into my nostril! I had to use tweezers to remove the hull from my nose. Don't get me started about the smell of the birdcage, either. Even though I changed the paper every day, I went through an entire bottle of my favorite perfume from Paris, France."

Mrs. Blinkhorn thought it best to refrain from making further suggestions for the upcoming ball. To make conversation, Mrs. Blinkhorn mentioned that she noticed the colorful array of red, orange, yellow, and purple tulips that had recently sprouted in Mrs. Paddington's garden.

"That's it!" Mrs. Paddington exclaimed, almost jumping out of the chair, "I loved my visit to Holland last year. I love their adorable wooden shoes. But they look most uncomfortable. I can't imagine walking around in them. Of course, I love their tulips, too. Unfortunately, Mrs. Priscilla Abernathy wore a pair of wooden shoes with a tulip decoration to last month's ball, so I can't use them in my hair. Instead, I want you to create a hairdo with a windmill, yes, a *windmill*, in my hair."

For the next several hours, Mrs. Blinkhorn fussed and fussed to create the perfect hairstyle for the ball. A wire frame was used to start her sculpture, or rather the towering hair creation that would sit upon Mrs. Muriel Paddington's head. A small pillow stuffed with horse hair and wool was set into place. Next, Mrs. Blinkhorn reached for a large bag on the table containing hair extensions.

"I am so lucky that my maid, Carista, offered to donate her long hair as extensions for my hairdo," smiled Mrs. Paddington.

Donated was not the word that Mrs. Blinkhorn would have used. The young maid cried and cried earlier in the day as Mrs. Blinkhorn cut off her long locks. The bag also contained some hair from Mrs. Paddington's pet poodle, Sassafras. All the hair would be used to help create the towering three-foot-tall hairdo, so popular for wealthy women in the 18th century.

Mrs. Paddington's eyes got heavy and she nodded off for a bit. Mrs. Blinkhorn added a brightly painted windmill to the hair. Mrs. Blinkhorn stifled a giggle as she saw the exhales of loud snores from her client cause the windmill to actually spin!

To help style the hair, a sticky **pomade** of beef-marrow and wax was rubbed over the hair. Mrs. Blinkhorn then dusted the hair with lilac colored flour. "It's amazing that Mrs. Paddington uses about one pound of flour each week, in her hair," Mrs. Blinkhorn thought to herself.

A strong wind from the open window blew some of the lilac powder onto Mrs. Blinkhorn's face, hair and apron. Some even covered her black buckled shoes a shade of bright lilac. "It's no wonder most elegant homes have 'powder rooms' where this can be done without the flour getting all over the place," thought the hairdresser.

Mrs. Blinkhorn stopped to gaze at her work of art and thought to herself that she indeed was a very talented hairdresser.

Finished with her masterpiece, Mrs. Blinkhorn woke
Mrs. Paddington who was delighted with the results. "I just
need to add a mixture of sugar water to make everything stay
nice and firm," explained Mrs. Blinkhorn.

"Oh, my, you did a wonderful job with my hair! Thank you ever so much," smiled a grateful Mrs. Paddington. "Maybe, I will win the contest for most beautiful hair at the Moonlight Ball."

Mrs. Paddington paid the hairdresser and rang the bell for her maid to escort Mrs. Blinkhorn to the door. With tears still streaming down her face, and wearing a scarf to cover her short hair, Carista came to get Mrs. Blinkhorn. Calling out a "good luck at the Moonlight Ball" to Mrs. Paddington, the hairdresser left.

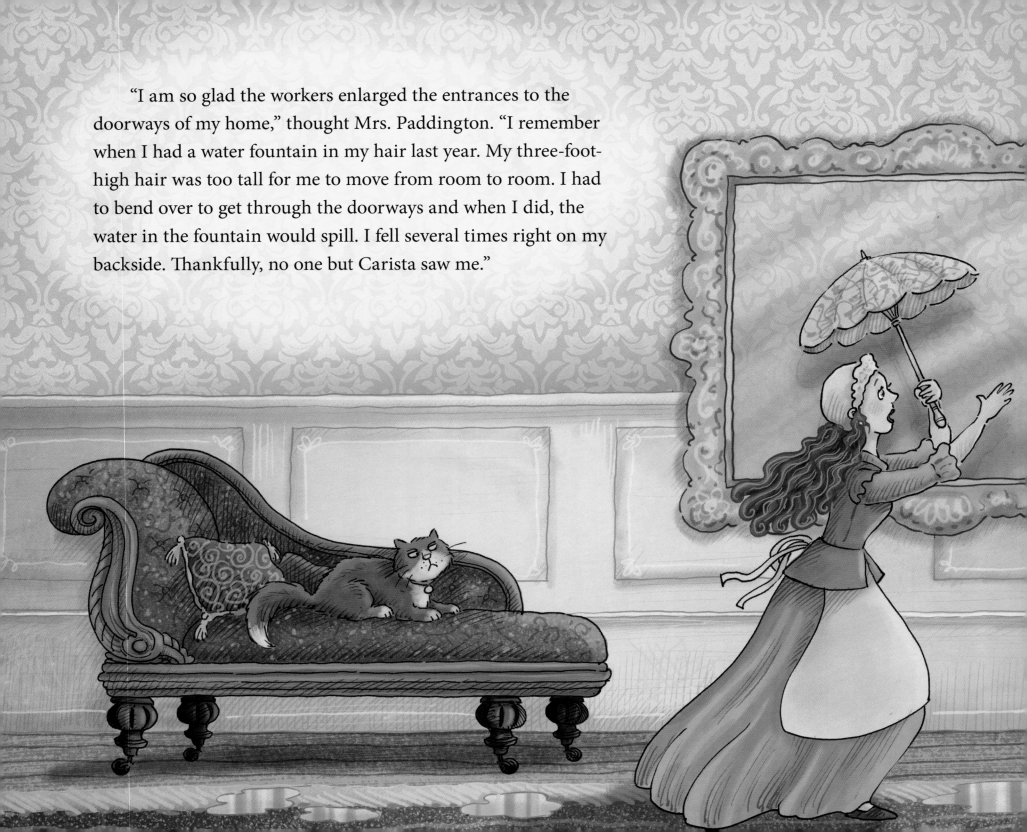

"I am so glad the workers enlarged the entrances to the doorways of my home," thought Mrs. Paddington. "I remember when I had a water fountain in my hair last year. My three-foot-high hair was too tall for me to move from room to room. I had to bend over to get through the doorways and when I did, the water in the fountain would spill. I fell several times right on my backside. Thankfully, no one but Carista saw me."

That night, Mrs. Paddington got ready for bed. Because she was very tired, she had difficultly standing straight up with the weight of her hair. The weight gave her a terrific headache. Removing her shoes took almost an hour. The challenge was to balance the windmill on her head while reaching down to her shoes. Next, changing into her nightgown took nearly another hour. Mrs. Paddington carefully got into bed and plumped up the special pillow that had an opening for her neck so her hair wouldn't get flattened. "It is most uncomfortable what a lady must do to look beautiful," sighed Mrs. Paddington.

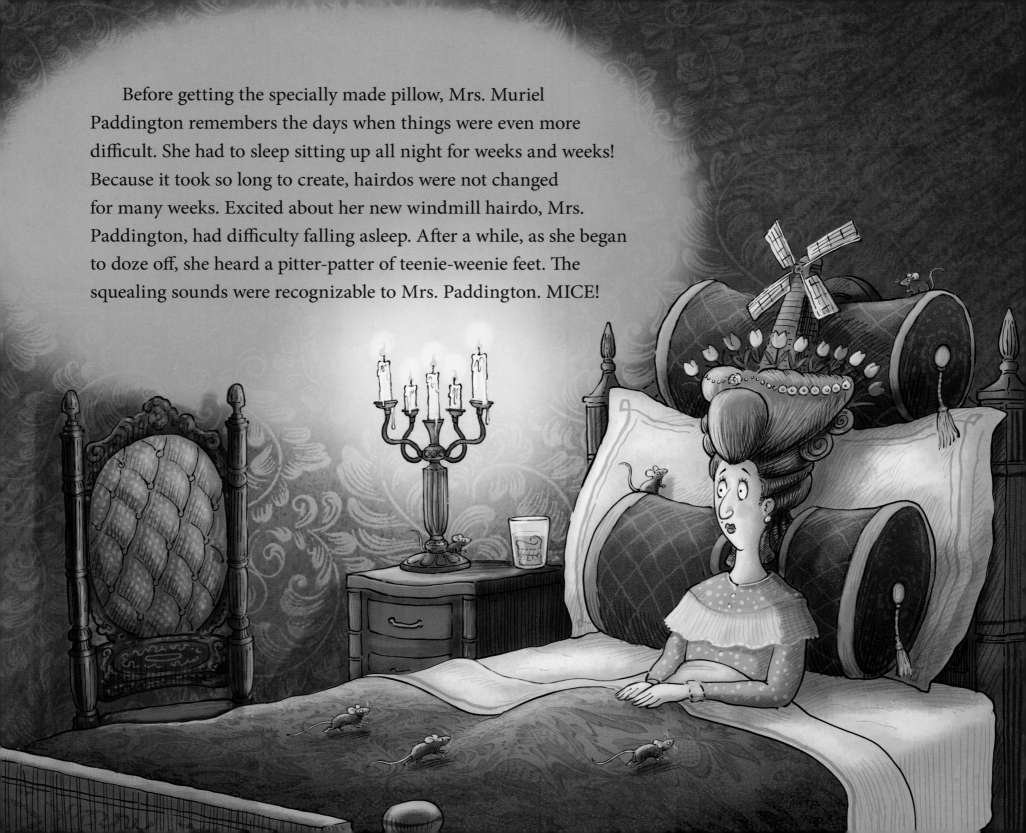

Before getting the specially made pillow, Mrs. Muriel
Paddington remembers the days when things were even more
difficult. She had to sleep sitting up all night for weeks and weeks!
Because it took so long to create, hairdos were not changed
for many weeks. Excited about her new windmill hairdo, Mrs.
Paddington, had difficulty falling asleep. After a while, as she began
to doze off, she heard a pitter-patter of teenie-weenie feet. The
squealing sounds were recognizable to Mrs. Paddington. MICE!

"Oh, dear," Mrs. Paddington said aloud. "I so dislike mice. I guess it is the dried sugar water in my hair that is attracting them again. And, I suppose the smell of the beef marrow, too." She remembered last month while visiting Mrs. Vivian Kindlesides for tea, a tiny black mouse jumped out of her hair and into Mrs. Kindlesides' teacup. It was horrible and terribly embarrassing. Mrs. Kindlesides calmly suggested Mrs. Paddington make a discreet visit to a shop, near Lincoln's Inn Field, London's largest public square. The place to go, she said is the Silver Mousetrap Shoppe. Mrs. Kindlesides said it has been around since 1690 and that she and many of her friends had made special purchases at the store. "I need to go to the Silver Mousetrap Shoppe tomorrow," Mrs. Paddington said with conviction.

The SILVER MOUSETRAP

Est. 1690

Mousetraps and Jewelry

The Silver Mousetrap in Lincoln's Inn Field in London actually existed. It was a jewelry store called A. Woodhouse & Son. The building still stands today with the sign advertising one of their popular products.

The next morning, Mrs. Muriel Paddington summoned her carriage
driver, Drummel Peachornby, to take her to Carney Street in London, near
the Royal Courts of Justice. Her destination was the Silver Mousetrap Shoppe.
As she tried to step into the carriage, she realized she had a problem. Her
hair was too high for her to get into her carriage! "What am I to do," she
wondered aloud. "I must get to the Silver Mousetrap today!" With no other
ideas, she contorted her body into the carriage but not her head. There was no
other way. Directing Peachornby to drive extremely slowly, she rode the entire
way with her head and hair sticking out of the window!

Upon reaching the Silver Mousetrap Shoppe, Drummel Peachornby opened the carriage door and Mrs. Paddington, with hardly a hair out of place, exited the carriage.

The tinkling of a sterling silver bell on the door signaled to the jewelry store owner that a customer had entered. The owner, Mr. Thomas Berryworth, looked but saw no one. Poor Mrs. Paddington couldn't get inside because her hair was far too tall for the height of the doorway entrance. She had to get on her hands and knees and crawl through the door, most unladylike for sure!

On entering the shop, Mr. Berryworth, helped Mrs. Paddington to her feet. Mr. Thomas Berryworth, didn't say so, but he was very accustomed to this manner of women entering his establishment. "Good day, my good woman. And how may I help you today?"

"You see, well, I, well," Mrs. Paddington stammered. "I, I, how do I say this…"

Thomas Berryworth shook his head knowingly. Actually, his elegant sterling silver mousetraps were often purchased by women with the popular tall hairstyles. "I have had many women with your problem come to my shoppe. What you are trying to say, if I might finish your sentence, is that you are in need of several sterling silver mousetraps."

"Oh, yes, thank you ever so much. Because it takes so very long to get my hair to look like this, I wait weeks before I wash my hair! The sugar water and beef marrow attract those pesky rodents," explained Mrs. Paddington.

Mr. Thomas Berryworth observed his customer's hairdo. "The red windmill is most unusual." At this point the windmill began to spin and spin.

"Dear me, I am a bit dizzy. And, the weight of the heavy windmill is giving me a horrible headache. Might I sit down for a bit and could I trouble you for a glass of water?" asked Mrs. Paddington.

Thomas Berryworth got a chair for Mrs. Muriel Paddington who promptly took a seat. He then fetched water and served it in a beautiful crystal goblet. As the windmill's spinning began to slow, eventually coming to a stop, she felt much better.

"Here are three sterling silver mousetraps," beamed Thomas Berryworth, counting silently the money he would earn from the sale. "Set the traps around your head this evening before you go to sleep. But, do be very careful. If you should have a bad dream and your arms begin to flail around, you might catch a finger in one of the traps!"

As Mrs. Muriel Paddington got up to leave, Mrs. Paddington unfastened a pewter headscratcher from her waist. Scratchers were a fashion accessory used by many wealthy women at the time. She began running the scratcher vigorously up and down her spine. "Oh my stars, I have such an itchy back. I imagine I spent too long in my garden yesterday pruning my prize roses and must have gotten a bit of a sunburn."

Mr. Berryworth turned his back to stifle a laugh. He knew that wasn't the reason for Mrs. Paddington's itchy back. He could see a small army of tiny bugs scurrying from her hairdo straight down her back! It was a common sight with his clients that wore the high hairstyles.

Scratch that itch!

In the 18th and 19th Centuries, headscratchers made of whalebone, ivory or wood were common. They were often used for scratching the effects of lice and other insects. And women used them as a sort of long comb to keep their tall powdered hair in place.

Mrs. Muriel Paddington was forced once again to get down on hands and knees and crawl back out of the Silver Mousetrap Shoppe doorway onto Carney Street. As she exited the store, there was a tinkling of the sterling silver bell on the front door to the shoppe. Mrs. Paddington, still on the ground, met Priscilla Abernathy, also crawling on hands and knees, coming into the Silver Mousetrap Shoppe. As both women passed each other, they made pleasantries and said they looked forward to the ball on Saturday evening. Thankfully, a thoughtful Thomas Berryworth had installed rugs at the entrance to his shoppe for the clients entering in such an unusual way!

Once outside the shoppe, her driver, Drummel Peachornby, helped her into the carriage as best as he could. Once again, Mrs. Paddington went home with her head sticking out of the window. As the carriage clattered through the streets of London, several children spotted the most unusual sight. Laughter filled the air and Mrs. Muriel Paddington could hear the sounds of giggles.

"I don't care," she thought, trying to look proud. Although it wasn't possible to look proud with her head sticking out of the carriage! "I have an important ball to attend tomorrow and I must look my very best. Besides, I hope I may win the contest for the most beautifully designed hair."

Vive la France

One of the most fashionable hairstyles of the eighteenth century in Paris, À la Belle Poule, represented the victory of a French ship over an English ship in 1778. The hair was decorated with a model of the Belle Poule ship, including sails and flags.

That evening after spending hours removing her shoes and changing into her nightgown, Mrs. Muriel Paddington carefully set the three silver mousetraps around the pillow where her head would lie. Exhausted, she then climbed into bed. She was excited about tomorrow night's ball and seeing all her friends and their fancy hair styles. She remembered last month's hair contest went to Mrs. Lafayette, for a ship in her hair celebrating the 1778 victory of the French **frigate**, *Belle Poule*, over the British. "Personally, I didn't think it was in good taste to award someone who was celebrating a French victory over the British, but I didn't wish to look like a sore loser," remembered Mrs. Paddington.

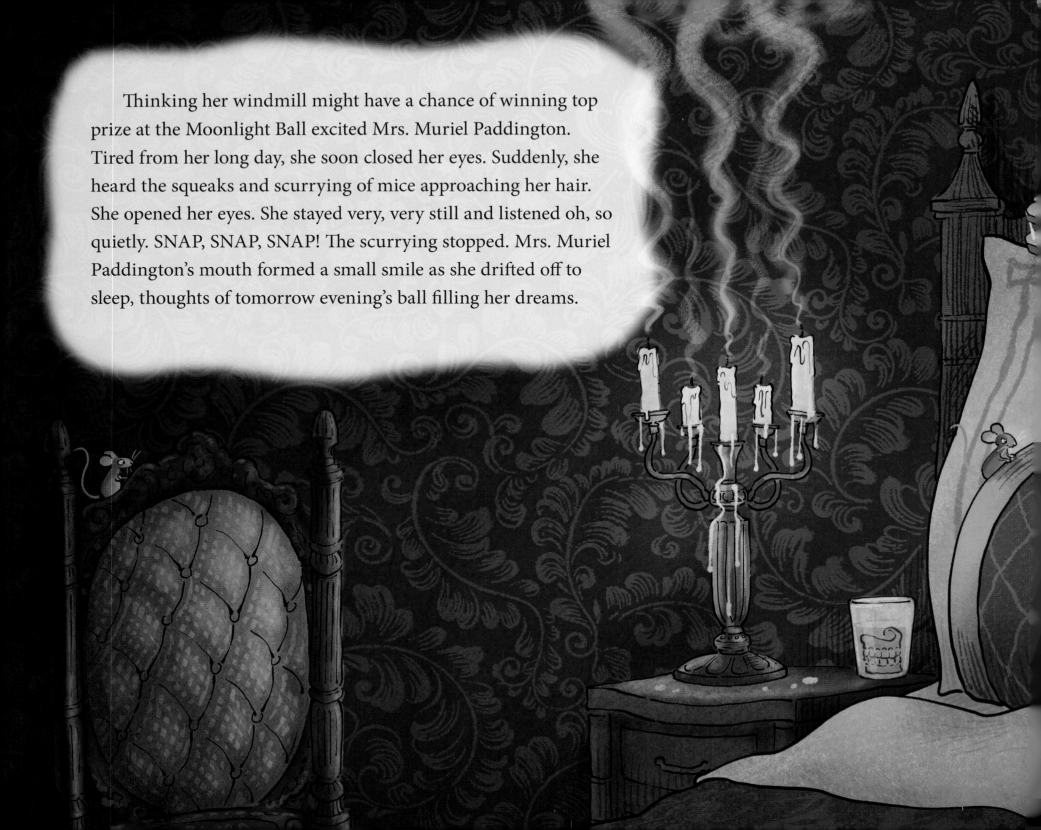

Thinking her windmill might have a chance of winning top prize at the Moonlight Ball excited Mrs. Muriel Paddington. Tired from her long day, she soon closed her eyes. Suddenly, she heard the squeaks and scurrying of mice approaching her hair. She opened her eyes. She stayed very, very still and listened oh, so quietly. SNAP, SNAP, SNAP! The scurrying stopped. Mrs. Muriel Paddington's mouth formed a small smile as she drifted off to sleep, thoughts of tomorrow evening's ball filling her dreams.

Sources:

London's Strangest Tales by Tom Quinn (Pavilion, 2018)

Fashions in Hair by Richard Corson (Peter Owen Publishers, 2005)

History of Fashion by J. Anderson Black (Black Cat, 1990)

Publisher's Cataloging-In-Publication Data
(Prepared by The Donohue Group, Inc.)

Names: Hennessey, Gail Skroback, 1951- author. | Cox, Steve, 1961- illustrator.

Title: Mrs. Paddington and the silver mousetraps : a hair-raising history of women's hairstyles in 18th-century London / written by Gail Skroback Hennessey ; illustrated by Steve Cox.

Description: [South Egremont, Massachusetts] : Red Chair Press, [2020] | Interest age level: 008-012. | Summary: A fictional account of the towering hairstyles that women wore in 18th century England.

Identifiers: ISBN 9781634409001 (library hardcover) | ISBN 9781634409018 (ebook PDF) | ISBN 9781634409025 (ePub)

Subjects: LCSH: Hairstyles--England--London--History--18th century--Juvenile fiction. | London (England)--Social life and customs--18th century--Juvenile fiction. | CYAC: Hairstyles--England--London--History--18th century--Fiction. | London (England)--Social life and customs--18th century--Fiction.

Classification: LCC PZ7.H391468 Mr 2020 (print) | LCC PZ7.H391468 (ebook) | DDC [Fic]--dc23

LC record available at https://lccn.loc.gov/2019933547

Photo credits: p. 21: © Mike Quinn/geograph.org.uk; p. 36: © Florilegius/Alamy Stock Photo

Printed in the United States of America

0419 1P S20

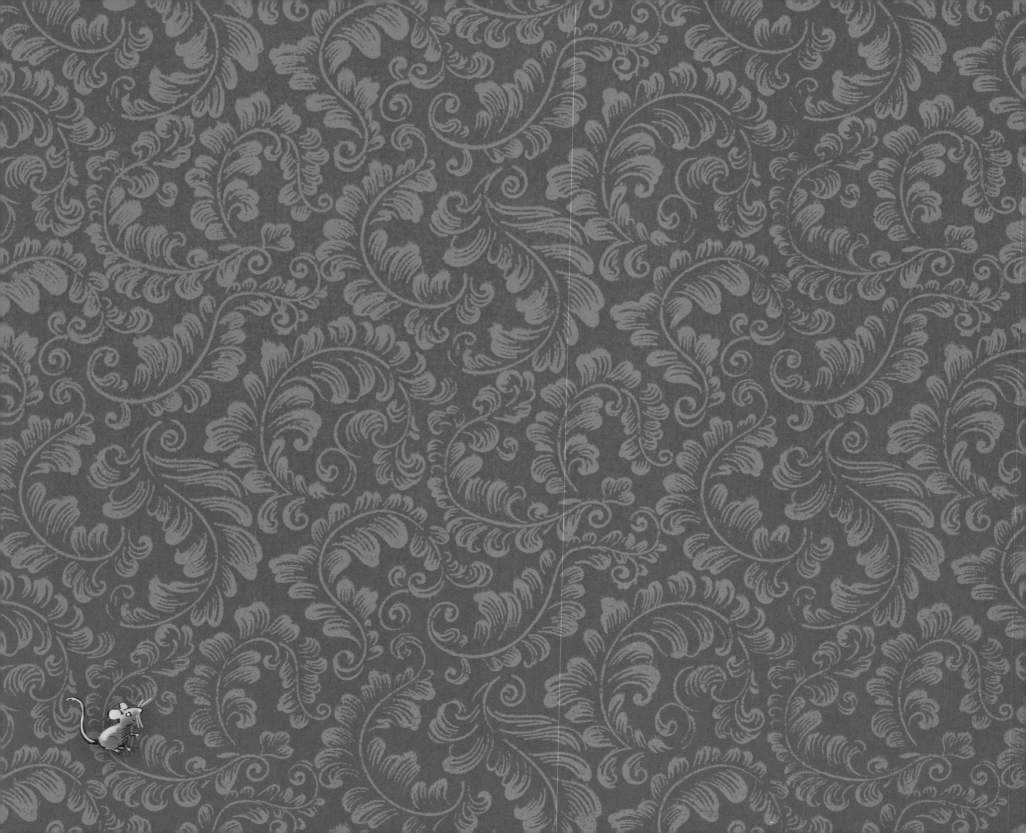